Anya
the Cuddly
Creatures
Fairy

Special thanks to Rachel Elliot

No part of this publication may be reproduced, stored in a retrieval system, or transmitted in any form or by any means, electronic, mechanical, photocopying, recording, or otherwise, without written permission of the publisher. For information regarding permission, write to Rainbow Magic Limited c/o HIT Entertainment, 830 South Greenville Avenue, Allen, TX 75002-3320.

ISBN 978-0-545-43392-1

12 11 10 9 8 7 6 5 4 3 2 1   12 13 14 15 16 17/0

Printed in China   68

First Scholastic printing, August 2012

Anya
the Cuddly Creatures Fairy

by Daisy Meadows

SCHOLASTIC INC.

New York   Toronto   London   Auckland

Sydney   Mexico City   New Delhi   Hong Kong

Jack Frost's
Ice Castle

Bus

Croquet

Playground

The Golden Palace

door Theater

The fairies are planning a magical ball,
With guests of honor and fun for all.
They're expecting a night full of laughter and cheer,
But they'll get a shock when my goblins appear!

Adventures and treats will be things of the past,
And I'll beat those troublesome fairies at last.
My iciest magic will blast through the room
And the world will be plunged into grimness
and gloom!

Contents

Sunshine at the Golden Palace

"Another perfect day!" said Rachel Walker happily. She was standing in the sunshine on the grand entrance steps of the Golden Palace. Rachel's best friend, Kirsty Tate, looked up at the sky and smiled as the bright sunbeams warmed her face.

"It's royal weather for a royal palace!" Kirsty agreed.

Kirsty and Rachel were staying at the Golden Palace for a special Royal Sleepover Camp for kids over spring vacation. Today, Kirsty's mother was bringing Kirsty's younger cousin Charlie to spend the day with them.

"I'm looking forward to showing Charlie all the amazing places here," said Kirsty. "I wonder what he'll like best. The drawbridge? The moat?"

"Or the petting zoo, the magic staircases, the dungeons, or the maze," said Rachel, counting them off on her fingers. "There are so many things to show him, I don't think one day will be enough!"

"Staying here really does make me feel like a princess," Kirsty said, gazing out across the palace gardens.

"How about a Princess Fairy?" Rachel asked.

The girls shared a secret smile. They were friends with the fairies who lived in Fairyland, and they often helped them when Jack Frost and his goblins caused trouble. At the moment, the fairies needed their help more than ever before. When the girls had arrived at the Golden Palace, they had been invited to a special ball in Fairyland in honor of the Princess Fairies. But Jack Frost had crashed the party and stolen the princesses' tiaras!

"Jack Frost is so mean," said Kirsty, thinking about the cold-hearted master of the Ice Castle. "The Princess Fairies need their tiaras to make sure that humans and fairies can have a happy, magical time. Without them, there will be problems all over the human world and in Fairyland."

"We've already found two of the tiaras," Rachel reminded her best friend.

"And we know that the others are somewhere at the Golden Palace. I'm sure we'll find them!" Queen Titania had not been able to keep Jack Frost from taking the tiaras to the human world, but she had cast a spell to make sure that the tiaras would all end up at the Golden Palace. That way, Rachel and Kirsty could help get them back!

Before the girls could say another word about Fairyland or the tiaras, they saw Mrs. Tate's car driving over the drawbridge and pulling up in front of the palace.

"Hi, Mom!" called Kirsty, waving. "Hi, Charlie!"

A very excited-looking little boy climbed out of the car.

"Hi, Kirsty!" he called at the top of his voice. "Hi, Rachel! This place is AMAZING!"

Mrs. Tate hugged Kirsty and Rachel.

"Are you having a good time, girls?" she asked.

"Oh, yes!" Rachel exclaimed. "It's even more exciting here than we imagined!"

"We want to show Charlie the petting zoo and the royal stables," said Kirsty eagerly. Just then, Mrs. Tate cried out. One of the palace peacocks had jumped up onto a stone pedestal and started pecking at her purse!

"Shoo!" said Rachel, flapping her arms at the peacock.

The peacock lifted its tail feathers and stalked away. Kirsty and Rachel stared at it with astonishment.

"I've never seen a peacock act like that before!" said Kirsty, frowning.

"Me, neither," Rachel added.

"Maybe there's something in the air," said Mrs. Tate. "Kirsty's cat, Pearl, has been out of sorts, too. She's

been running away and hiding all morning."

"That's really strange," said Kirsty, frowning. "Pearl usually loves curling up in people's laps."

"Maybe she misses you," said Charlie.

"I wonder if Buttons misses *me*," said Rachel, thinking of her shaggy dog.

"I'm sure he does," said Mrs. Tate. "I have to go now, but I'll be back to pick you up this afternoon, Charlie. Bye, girls!"

She got into her car and waved her hand out the window as she drove away.

When the car had disappeared over the drawbridge, Kirsty turned to Charlie with a big smile.

"What would you like to see first, Charlie," she said, "the maze or the petting zoo?"

"Oooh, I want to see the animals!" said Charlie, his eyes shining with delight. "I love animals!"

Pony Pandemonium

Rachel and Kirsty led Charlie to the playground behind the palace. Charlie gasped when he saw the tall climbing wall in the center.

"That's called Rapunzel's Tower," Rachel explained.

"I definitely want to explore that later!" Charlie declared.

They passed the Snow White
playhouse, walked around the lake, and
finally arrived at the little petting zoo.
Charlie smiled happily when he saw
the pigpen, the goat enclosure, and the
rabbit hutches.

Rachel crouched down beside a fluffy
white lop-eared rabbit. She saw a little
bucket full of salad scraps, and picked
out some lettuce for the rabbit.

"Would you like to feed him?" she
asked Charlie.

Charlie crouched down
beside her and held
out the lettuce. But
the rabbit turned
around and
hopped away!

Charlie's smile faded a little.

"Did I do something wrong?" he asked.

"Maybe he's not feeling very well," Kirsty suggested. "We should probably tell Jean, the animal keeper."

She looked around for Jean, but the only people in sight were five boys who were peeking into the henhouse. They were wearing stylish riding jackets and breeches, with tall boots and velvety riding hats. The brims of the hats hid their faces completely.

"No eggs in here!" one of the boys yelled.

Then Kirsty noticed something very strange.

"Rachel, look!" she said. "There are guinea pigs on top of the henhouse!"

Sure enough, several guinea pigs were now sitting on the henhouse roof. Kirsty and Rachel exchanged surprised glances.

Meanwhile, the boys had moved over to the rabbit hutches, and were trying to pet the rabbits. But every time they got close, the rabbits scattered.

"Come on," said Kirsty, seeing that Charlie was disappointed. "Let's visit the royal stables."

The girls led the way to the stables. They were surprised to see a beautiful golden carriage in the cobblestone courtyard outside. In the sunshine, the gold sparkled and glimmered like fairy dust.

Kirsty and Rachel peeked inside the carriage and saw soft, cushiony red seats with wide padded armrests.

"It looks magical," Rachel whispered in delight.

"Just like Cinderella's carriage," said Kirsty, smiling at her best friend.

Charlie was looking at some sacks of animal feed leaning against the wall. "Horse oats, chicken corn, and llama grain," he said, reading the labels aloud. "Each animal has its own special food."

Suddenly they heard a loud neighing and stomping.

"It's coming from that stall over there!" said Rachel, after looking around. "Come on!"

The girls and Charlie raced over to the stall, which had a brass plaque on the door:

My name is Duchess.
I am a Shetland pony.

Charlie and the girls peeked around the stable door. Inside, Jean the animal keeper was standing beside a pretty Shetland pony holding a grooming brush.

"Calm down,

Duchess," Jean was saying. "I'm just trying to help you look your best."

"Hello, Jean!" said Rachel. "We wanted to show Charlie the stables."

"I love ponies," said Charlie, running into the stall.

"Be careful!" warned Jean. "Duchess is in a very weird mood today."

Just then, Duchess gave a loud snort and broke away from Jean. She dashed past Charlie, knocking him into a pile of straw, and charged out into the courtyard.

"Duchess, stop!" Jean cried.

But Duchess was in a bad mood, and she wasn't listening. She kicked over the feed sacks that were stacked against the wall, and grain, corn, and oats poured out onto the cobblestones in the yard.

"Oh, Duchess!" exclaimed Jean. Charlie hid nervously behind Kirsty while Jean coaxed Duchess back into her stall and Rachel picked up the overturned sacks. At last, Jean came out and closed the stall door behind her.

"I don't know what's wrong with Duchess," she said. "She's usually such a friendly little pony. Today's camp activity is taking place in the barn—I hope she's in a better mood by then."

Rachel and Kirsty exchanged glances, both thinking the same thing. So many animals had been acting strangely this morning — could it have something to do with the Princess Fairies' missing tiaras?

Anya Appears!

Jean scooped some feed into a bucket and smiled at Charlie, who looked upset.

"Are you OK after your tumble in the straw?" Jean said, ruffling Charlie's hair. "I'm sorry about Duchess. Would you like to come and help me feed some of the other animals?"

"Yes, please!" Charlie cried excitedly.

"Maybe you can try to get the guinea pigs to come down from the henhouse," Jean added. "They've been up there all morning."

Charlie rushed ahead with Jean following him. Rachel and Kirsty were about to join them when they heard a gentle whinny. They looked around and saw a tall white stallion looking out from a nearby stall.

"What a beautiful horse!" Rachel exclaimed. The horse whinnied again, and nodded his head a couple times. "It's almost as if

he's trying to get our attention," said
Kirsty. "Come on, let's go and say hello
to him."

The nameplate on the horse's stall said
MERLIN.

"Hello, Merlin," said Rachel, reaching
up and petting his soft nose.

Then she noticed something strange.
"Look, Kirsty!" Rachel said, pointing to
the top of Merlin's head.

As the girls watched,
a tiny sparkling
light gradually
grew brighter.
Then Princess
Anya the
Cuddly Creatures
Fairy peeked
through Merlin's silvery mane!

"Princess Anya!" cried Kirsty in delight.

"Hello, Kirsty! Hello, Rachel," said the Princess Fairy, flashing a dazzling smile as she flipped her braid over her shoulder. She was wearing an orange dress with animal-print trim. "I've come to check on the animals! I'm happy to see that my friend Merlin seems fine. Have you seen any of the other animals?"

"Yes, we have," said Rachel. "Princess Anya, I think Jack Frost's horrible plan is working! A peacock tried to peck Kirsty's mom's purse, the rabbits didn't want any food, the hens haven't laid any eggs, and the guinea pigs are on top of the henhouse!"

"And Duchess the pony is in a very bad mood," added Kirsty. "We wondered if it had anything to do with the missing tiaras."

"I'm afraid it does." Anya sighed sadly. "Without my tiara, I can't watch over the special friendships that exist between animals and humans. That's why the animals have been behaving so strangely. I even had to leave my own little Bengal kitten in Fairyland, in case she's affected."

"We have to

find that tiara," said Kirsty in a determined voice.

But Rachel was confused. "Why is Merlin still in a good mood?" she asked Anya.

The fairy's eyes sparkled as she smiled. "He's my special animal friend," she explained. "He's descended from the very first horses that lived at the Golden Palace hundreds of years ago. They carried knights in armor, and Merlin remembers all the stories that have been passed down through his family."

Rachel patted Merlin's warm neck and stroked his silky mane. He gently nuzzled her shoulder.

"It seems like Merlin is the only animal who still has a special bond with people," Anya said. "Will you take me to see the other animals, girls?"

"Of course," said Kirsty. "You'd better hide, though, Princess Anya."

Rachel held open her jacket pocket so that Anya could fly into it. The girls said good-bye to Merlin and walked toward the petting zoo.

As they drew closer, they heard loud bangs and shouts. When they reached the zoo, they stared in astonishment.

The five boys they had seen earlier were running between the animal hutches and pens, shouting to one another as they ran. Two of them were overturning bales of hay, and the others were looking under water troughs and emptying feed buckets. They seemed to be in a panic, and were terrifying the rabbits, guinea pigs, and hens. The animals had all raced to their homes in fright.

Charlie dashed over to the girls with a sad, worried look on his face. "Why are those big boys being so mean?" he asked. "The animals will never be brave enough to come out of their pens now!" At that moment, Jean the animal keeper marched toward the boys, looking very angry. "Leave the zoo right now!" she ordered. "You're upsetting all the animals."

The boys stomped past Rachel and

Kirsty, grumbling to themselves.

"We've got to find it—it must be here somewhere!" the girls heard the tallest boy say.

"What a funny voice that boy has," Rachel noticed.

"And they all have very big feet for their height. . . ." added Kirsty.

The girls gasped and turned to face each other.

"Kirsty—they're goblins!" Rachel whispered in alarm.

"Yes," said Kirsty. "And it sounds like they're looking for something. It must be Anya's tiara!"

Llama Drama

Jean offered to take Charlie to the
playground. What a relief! Now Rachel
and Kirsty could talk to Anya. They
knew Charlie wouldn't enjoy the petting
zoo while the animals were behaving so
strangely, so he wasn't missing anything.

As soon as Charlie and Jean were
out of sight, Anya flew out of Rachel's
pocket.

"Those awful goblins!" Anya exclaimed. "How dare they frighten all the animals like that?"

"At least we know that the tiara is somewhere in the petting zoo," said Kirsty. "The goblins must have dropped it here."

"Quick, let's search for it before they come back," said Rachel eagerly.

"It will be easier for you to look if you're the same size as me," said Anya.

Rachel and Kirsty held hands as Anya waved her wand. A ribbon of glittering gold whirled from the tip of her wand

and wound itself into a circle above
them. Then it burst
like a tiny
firework,
showering
Rachel and
Kirsty in
silvery
sparkles. They
instantly shrank
to fairy-size and
found themselves hovering beside Anya,
fluttering their silvery wings.

The girls started their search in
the henhouse, where Rachel noticed
something immediately.

"The hen in the far corner is sitting on
something golden!" she exclaimed. "It
must be the tiara!"

They flew toward the reddish-brown hen. She clucked at them in surprise.

"Excuse me, do you have my golden tiara?" asked Anya politely.

The hen moved slightly, and the girls saw that she was sitting on a bunch of tiny golden chicks. Although they were very sweet, the girls still felt disappointed.

"Let's keep searching," said Anya.

They flew through a wooden gate into the goat pen. At once, they realized they were right under the nose of a young billy goat. The goat glared at them and

lowered his head.

"Look out!" cried Rachel as the goat
charged at them.

The fairies scattered in three different
directions, and the billy goat thundered
past.

"That was close!" said Kirsty,
hovering out of reach.

"I don't think the tiara is here," said Princess Anya. "The goblins would have been too scared of that billy goat to enter the pen!"

They left the goat still charging around in circles, and fluttered into the rabbit hutches. A soft gray rabbit with fluffy ears stared at them in surprise. Kirsty reached out her hand to touch it, but the rabbit turned around and jumped into a pile of straw. All the girls could see was its quivering fluffy white tail. The girls and Anya searched through the hutches, but all they could find were old lettuce leaves and pieces of straw.

Suddenly a ray of sunshine filtered into the hutch and made something in the far corner flash gold.

"Over here!" cried Kirsty in excitement.

The girls eagerly pulled aside the straw, but all they found was a chunk of golden- yellow corn.

"It's no use," said Princess Anya, fluttering sadly to the ground. "We'll never find the tiara."

Rachel and Kirsty fluttered down, too, and put their arms around the princess's shoulders.

"Don't give up," said Rachel. "We've

already found two of the missing tiaras, and we'll find yours, too, I promise."

"With all three of us searching, we can't fail," added Kirsty. "Jack Frost is *not* going to get away with this!"

Princess Anya looked more cheerful. "I'm so glad you're here to help me!" she said. The three fairies flew over the fence and found themselves in front of the llama pasture. Kirsty gave a cry of surprise as she spotted the five goblins sneaking in through the gate!

"Maybe they remembered where they

lost the tiara," said Rachel. "Come on,
let's follow them!"

The three girls zipped along after the
goblins, staying close to the ground so
that the goblins wouldn't spot them. The
llamas were all in one corner, feeding
from a large trough.

"Out of my way, Hairy," snapped the
tallest goblin, shoving a cream-colored
llama aside.

"Move over, Big Neck," shouted a second goblin, who was wearing his riding hat backward.

He elbowed his way past a chocolate-colored llama. The other goblins scrambled forward, too, plunging their greedy green fingers into the trough and scraping out handfuls of llama grain. They seemed to be searching to see if anything was at the bottom of the trough.

"Those poor llamas!" said Kirsty under her breath.

"Don't worry," said Princess Anya with a little smile. "Llamas won't stand for being pushed around."

The llamas were already snorting with annoyance. Their food was being trampled into the ground by big goblin

feet! The chocolate-colored llama butted
one of the goblins
and sent him
headfirst into
a hedge.

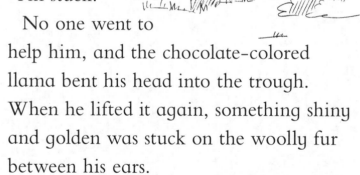

"Help!"
the goblin
squawked in a
muffled voice.
"I'm stuck!"

No one went to
help him, and the chocolate-colored
llama bent his head into the trough.
When he lifted it again, something shiny
and golden was stuck on the woolly fur
between his ears.

"My tiara!" Princess Anya gasped.

A Trough and a Tiara

Unfortunately, the goblins had noticed the tiara, too.

"GIVE ME THAT!" yelled the tallest of the goblins.

He snatched at it, but the llama gave a loud snort and bolted away from the trough. Startled, the other llamas followed him and thundered across the pasture at top speed.

"Catch them!" shouted the goblin. "Stop those horrible hairy beasts!"

The goblins started to chase the llamas, stumbling over weeds and roots. But their yelps and shouts only made the llamas run faster.

"They're too fast for the goblins," said Rachel.

"Yes, and they're too fast for us, too," said Princess Anya. "How can we make them come back?"

The girls thought hard.

"Maybe we could lure them back with some food?" Kirsty suggested after a moment.

They darted over to the trough, but it was empty.

"Do you remember the sacks that Duchess kicked over, Kirsty?" said Rachel. "Wasn't one of them full of llama grain?"

"Yes!" Kirsty exclaimed. "Good memory, Rachel. Come on!"

They flew out of the pasture, through the petting zoo, and

into the cobblestone courtyard of the stables. The sack of llama grain was still there — but it was a hundred times bigger than the fairies!

"It's much too heavy for us to carry very far," said Rachel. "We're going to have to change back to our normal size," Kirsty said.

"But it will take us too long to carry it all the way to the pasture," Rachel insisted. "The goblins might grab the tiara before we get back."

"What are we going to do?" asked Princess Anya in a panic.

At that moment, a loud neigh echoed

through the yard. Merlin's handsome
white head was poking out of his stall.

He neighed again, and a big smile
spread over Anya's face.

"Of course!" she said. "Merlin wants
to help us!"

She touched her wand to the
stall door and it
sprang open.
Merlin trotted
out, his hooves
clattering over
the cobblestones.

"Merlin can
carry the sack
to the pasture in
no time!" said Princess Anya. "We just
have to lift it onto his back."

Rachel and Kirsty each took a top

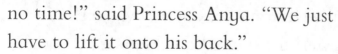

corner of the sack, and Princess Anya
grabbed the middle. On the count
of three, they all rose into the air,
fluttering their delicate wings as hard as
they could.

"Keep going!" Rachel puffed.
"Not—much—farther!"

The bag seemed to
get heavier
and heavier.
But at last,
with a final
heave, they managed
to lift the sack of
grain onto Merlin's
broad, strong back. Then they clutched
his silvery mane, and he was off!

Merlin cantered quickly back through
the petting zoo to the llama pasture.

The surprised faces of goats, pigs, and rabbits were a blur as he raced toward the pasture fence. Then he gave a loud whinny.

"Hold on tight!" cried Princess Anya.

The girls wound their tiny hands into the horse's silky mane, and Merlin soared over the fence. He landed on the soft grass of the pasture.

The llamas had gathered together in a corner of the pasture, facing off with four of the goblins, who were all flushed and panting. The goblins looked very, very angry, but the llamas looked even angrier. They hadn't enjoyed being chased by the goblins, and since Anya didn't have her tiara, they were feeling even grumpier than usual.

As the girls watched, the goblins slowly

started to move forward. The llamas began to paw the ground, lowering their woolly heads.

"Those goblins had better watch out," said Rachel. "It looks like the llamas are about to charge!"

Just as she finished speaking, the llamas ran at the goblins — who screeched in terror as they scattered around the pasture!

"Quickly, Merlin, go up to the llamas!" said Princess Anya.

Merlin moved toward the llamas, while Princess Anya, Rachel, and Kirsty pulled open the sack of feed. The llamas didn't seem to notice them. But then Anya waved her wand over the food, sprinkling it with golden sparkles. A delicious aroma rose from the sack, and the llamas paused and sniffed the air. In the distance, the goblins leaped over the fence and vanished from sight.

"Over to the trough, Merlin!" cried Princess Anya.

Merlin trotted over to the trough, and the girls poured the grain into it. Within seconds, the llamas had stuck their heads greedily into the trough. The chocolate-colored llama was among them, still wearing the golden tiara.

Rachel breathed a huge sigh of relief. Their plan had worked! All they needed to do now was to lift the tiara from the llama's head. But then Kirsty gave a cry of alarm.

The goblin who had been stuck in the hedge had finally wriggled free, and now he was climbing onto the chocolate-colored llama's back!

A Royal Result

The llama gave a loud snort and kicked up his back legs, flinging the goblin into the air. The goblin landed on the back of the next llama, who did exactly the same thing . . . and the next . . . and the next!

"YEE-OUCH!" squawked the goblin, as he was bounced from llama to llama. "OOOH! OWWW! ARGH!"

Finally he toppled headfirst onto the ground, and lay there panting, sprawled in the mud.

As the chocolate-colored llama dipped his head down to eat again, Rachel gently took the tiara from his woolly head. She handed it to Princess Anya with a big smile. "We did it!" she said.

Princess Anya reached for the tiara, and it shrank to fairy-size again. She placed it back on top of her golden hair, where it shined as brightly as the sun.

"Girls, I will never forget what you did for me today," she said, smiling at them. "How can I ever thank you?"

"The best reward is seeing your tiara

back where it belongs," said Kirsty, giving Princess Anya a hug. "We're just happy that we found it!"

"Merlin helped, too," Rachel reminded her friend.

Princess Anya waved her wand and a large apple appeared in the air beside Merlin. As he crunched on it happily, Princess Anya waved her wand again so the girls returned to human-size.

"It's time for me to go back to Fairyland," Anya said. "I can't wait to tell the other princesses how wonderful you've been!"

She waved good-bye and then, in a shower of sparkly fairy dust, she was gone. Rachel and Kirsty chatted happily as they led Merlin back to the stables.

"We did it!" said Rachel. "Three of the missing tiaras are back with the princesses!"

"That leaves four still to find," Kirsty added.

"We'll find them," said Rachel in a determined voice. "I know we will!"

As they passed through the petting zoo, they saw Jean scratching her head. The girls hurried up to her.

"All the animals seem happy and friendly again," she said in a surprised voice. "It's like magic, as if this morning was just a bad dream!"

The girls shared a secret smile. This meant that Anya's tiara was already restoring the special bond between humans and animals!

"That's wonderful news," said Rachel.

"Charlie is on the playground," said Jean. "I said I would send you to get him. I'll take Merlin back to the barn—thanks for giving him a walk!"

When Rachel and Kirsty brought Charlie back to the petting zoo, he was overjoyed that the animals were back to normal. The rabbits let him pet their soft fur and feed them little treats. Charlie crouched down and held out a palm full of carrot tops while hens clucked happily around his feet. He petted the guinea pigs, fed the goats, and even went to see Duchess in her stall. He was a little bit

scared that she might knock him over again, but as soon as she saw him, she gave him a friendly nuzzle.

"I think she's saying sorry," said Rachel with a smile.

"You certainly made a lot of animal friends today, Charlie!" said Kirsty.

At that moment, Jean looked around the stable door.

"It's time for today's camp activity!" she said. "I think you'll enjoy it!"

Kirsty and Rachel walked out of Duchess's stall and looked around in delight. Merlin was standing in the middle of the courtyard, harnessed to the beautiful carriage they had seen earlier. All the other boys and girls were there, too.

"This is a genuine old royal carriage

that has been restored," Jean told them. "And Merlin will be happy to give everyone a ride in it!"

Rachel and Kirsty stroked Merlin's mane and then climbed into the carriage. With a proud whinny, the horse set off. Rachel sank back into the soft velvet seat with a giggle.

"I feel more like a real princess than ever!" she said happily.

"Me, too!" said Kirsty, gazing out of the carriage window at the peacocks, who all looked calm again. "Oh, Rachel, I can't wait to find out what our next magical adventure will be!"

THE PRINCESS FAIRIES

Rachel and Kirsty have helped Hope,
Cassidy, and Anya find their tiaras.
Now it's time for them to help

Elisa
the Royal Adventure Fairy!

Join their next adventure
in this special sneak peek. . . .

A Ghostly Surprise

"I wonder what adventures Louis and Caroline have planned for us tonight," said Kirsty Tate, smiling across the grand banquet table at her best friend, Rachel Walker.

It was spring vacation, and they were staying at the Golden Palace for the

Royal Sleepover Camp, a special week-long event for kids. Louis and Caroline were two of the palace's camp directors, and they had been looking after the kids all week, making sure the activities were fit for princes and princesses.

"I'm sure they've planned something wonderful," said Rachel, scraping the last bit of strawberry ice cream from her silver bowl.

The banquet hall looked very beautiful, decorated with lots of twinkling candles and lights. Kirsty gazed thoughtfully out the large round window at the end of the hall. It was twilight, but she could still see the silhouette of the palace's crumbling old tower. It looked majestic against the purple sky, and it was the only place that the campers were not allowed to go.

"I wish they would let us climb all the way up to the top of the tower," Kirsty said. "I'd love to explore up there!"

"It sounds kind of scary to me," said a girl named Victoria, who was sitting next to Kirsty. "I'm not very adventurous."

Rachel and Kirsty exchanged a secret smile. They'd already had plenty of adventures that week! They had been helping their friends the Princess Fairies get their magic tiaras back from Jack Frost and his goblins. So far, they had found the tiaras that belonged to Princess Hope the Happiness Fairy, Princess Cassidy the Costume Fairy, and Princess Anya the Cuddly Creatures Fairy. But there were still four more tiaras to find. . . .

RAINBOW magic™

There's Magic in Every Series!

The Rainbow Fairies
The Weather Fairies
The Jewel Fairies
The Pet Fairies
The Fun Day Fairies
The Petal Fairies
The Dance Fairies
The Music Fairies
The Sports Fairies
The Party Fairies
The Ocean Fairies
The Night Fairies
The Magical Animal Fairies
The Princess Fairies

Read them all!

■ SCHOLASTIC

www.scholastic.com
www.rainbowmagiconline.com

HiT entertainment

RMFAIR

RAINBOW magic™

SPECIAL EDITION

Three Books in Each One–More Rainbow Magic Fun!

 Joy the Summer Vacation Fairy

 Holly the Christmas Fairy

 Kylie the Carnival Fairy

 Stella the Star Fairy

 Shannon the Ocean Fairy

 Trixie the Halloween Fairy

 Gabriella the Snow Kingdom Fairy

 Juliet the Valentine Fairy

 Mia the Bridesmaid Fairy

 Flora the Dress-Up Fairy

 Paige the Christmas Play Fairy

 Emma the Easter Fairy

 Cara the Camp Fairy

 Destiny the Rock Star Fairy

 Belle the Birthday Fairy

 Olympia the Games Fairy

 Selena the Sleepover Fairy

 Cheryl the Christmas Tree Fairy

◼SCHOLASTIC

scholastic.com
rainbowmagiconline.com

 HiT entertainment

RMSPECIAL9

These activities are magical!
Play dress-up, send friendship notes, and much more!

SCHOLASTIC
www.scholastic.com
www.rainbowmagiconline.com

RMACTIV